D1450354

Copyright © 2020 Cynthia L. Hall

ISBN: 9798666828595

"constellation," *Merriam-Webster.com Dictionary*, https://www.merriam-webster.com/dictionary/constellation. Accessed 8/2/2020.

"Star." *Merriam-Webster.com Dictionary*, Merriam-Webster, https://www.merriam-webster.com/dictionary/star. Accessed 3 Aug. 2020.

Cover by
Interior Illustrations by Rashard Hollman
rashardhollman@yahoo.com

Editing by A. T. Destiny Awaits Group LLC
atdestinyawaitsgroup@gmail.com

DEDICATION

This Book is Dedicated to
My Children Tysonman, Edabee, Ivypooh, and my niece NeeNee!
Remember, whenever you are down, always look up!
I love you high as the sky,
Deep as the ocean,
And as wide as the sea.

ACKNOWLEDGMENTS

I cannot express enough thanks to my Head Start Preschool Family in Dothan, AL for giving me the opportunity for many years, to be an educator, incorporate my musical talents, to help inspire children to learn more, and help them grow intellectually.

A special thanks to my mom and grandmother for raising me, being affectionate, and making sure I had what I needed to grow and become the woman I am today. My mother and grandmother read to me and sang to me. That is the core of who I am and what I am most passionate about. I owe those passions to you beautiful, hard-working Queens. Thank you!

A huge thank you to my lil' big brother for being my very first best friend and continuing to make me very proud to be your big sis'!

Another huge thanks to my dad for always being extremely honest, even when it hurts. It was always needed, and as I have grown, I have learned to appreciate it. Thank you for being you!

Finally, a big thank you to my husband Ira Hall, close family, my sistar cousins, my sisies, and "freens" for always lifting my spirit, supporting, encouraging, and believing in me when we were up or down. More importantly, thank you 2020, despite the pandemic, for the birthing of strength, ideas, boldness, and talents I didn't know I had.

I am also grateful to my illustrator for being an awesome friend throughout the years and helping me with the vision of my book!

Ivyana had only one wish. It was more than a dream. Her eyes gazed into the night sky before bed every night.

Each night she would find a new constellation and try to name it, but it was always so hard to do.

She would always get lost in the stars and lose her spot connecting the stars to form a shape to name.

So, as usual, Ivyana went to bed one night and had a dream. Unknowingly, this dream would captivate her love for the night sky even more.

Early the following morning, she rose with such anticipation, determination, and excitement. As she began to get ready for school, she paused in thought as she was reflecting back on her dream,

...The dream that would put her name in the beautiful night sky. Her dream was to connect stars that would be in the shape of her name.

All-day-long, while Ivyana was in school, she daydreamed about seeing her name in the sky.

As the day came to an end, the sky grew darker and darker. The moon had taken its place in the sky. It was full and shining as bright as all the stars.

After dinner, Ivyana rushed quickly to her room to prepare for bed. As soon as she bathed, brushed her teeth and put on her pajamas; she would open her window and gaze into the night sky, knowing that tonight she would name her very own constellation.

After gazing a while, Ivyana was dizzy and closed her eyes to regroup. There were so many stars in the sky. Some big, some small, some twinkling, and some bright.

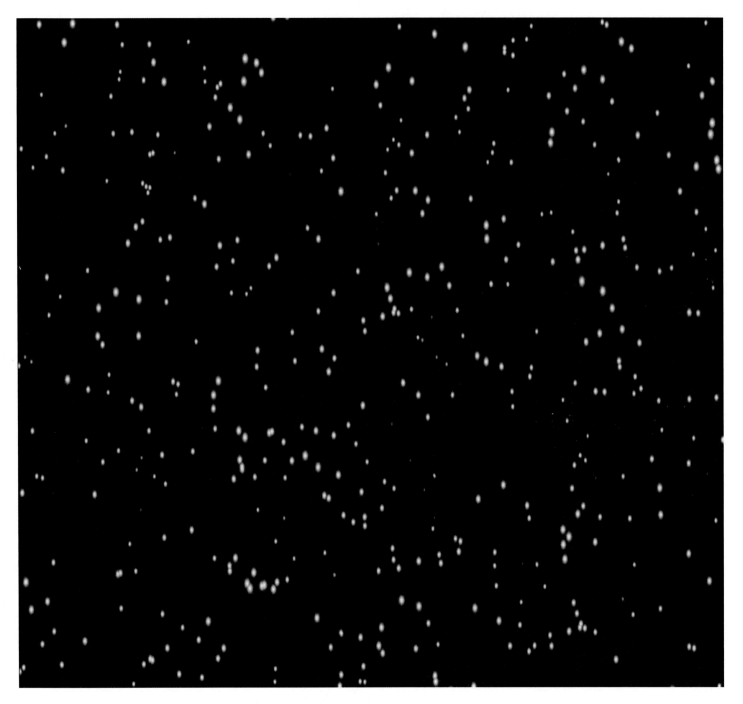

SO, she decided to take a deep breath.
She opened her eyes and
gazed into the stars again.
And there she saw it!

I...V...Y..A..N...A!

Every letter represented something
that is very special to her.

I- for Ice cream,
V- for Valentine's Day,
Y- for yo-yo,
A- for angel,
N- for necklace,
A- for an arrow going up!

The last A was very special to Ivyana.
The arrow up always inspired her
to look up, think, and believe.

Each star was a reason to look up, imagine, and dream. Every star seemed as if it was placed so gently... And now that her name was in the sky, she adored it nightly, still, and quiet.

After celebrating the moment that had finally come, she hurried to bed and waited patiently to dream of the night sky again, but this time with her name made of stars. She knew that every night for the rest of her life, she would see her own constellation.

The End

Glossary:

Constellation: A group of stars that forms a particular shape in the sky.

Star: any of the heavenly bodies except planets which are visible at night and look like fixed points of light

ABOUT THE AUTHOR

Cynthia Hall is a wife and mother of beautiful children. She has had the privilege of working at Early Head Start Preschool in Dothan, Alabama for several years as a Teacher's Assistant! She received two associate degrees in Early Childhood Education in 2011. There she realized certain gifts that would help in implementing different strategies that her students would benefit in learning. She also is a talented piano player whose journey started at the age of 11. She combines these passions as she continues to educate, inspire others, and remind all of us to look up!

Made in the USA
Coppell, TX
19 September 2020